The SHIP'S CAT and the SEA DOGS

Written by ANGELA HOLROYD • *Illustrated by* DAVID ANSTEY

To Anji

A TEMPLAR BOOK

Produced by The Templar Company plc,

Pippbrook Mill, London Road, Dorking, Surrey RH4 1JE, England

Designed by David Anstey and Mike Jolley

Printed and Bound in Italy

ISBN 1-898784-41-8

TEMPLAR

REWARD
for the capture of
MAD DOG
McNASTY
500 pieces of gold

Once there was a clever, hardworking cat called Jemima Sprat who scrimped and saved and finally collected enough money to buy a boat. She named her little ship *The Flipper*, and one fine morning she proudly set sail in her to fish the high seas.

Jemima found a good spot for fishing, lowered her sail and cast her net into the sea. Before long, the boat was overflowing with tasty fish.

She was just raising the sail ready to set off for home when, BOOM! There was a flash in the distance and seconds later a huge cannonball smashed straight through her little boat!

The Flipper sank almost immediately. Thrown overboard by the blast, Jemima just managed to climb onto a piece of floating wreckage before she was carried away by the waves.

She did not realize the pirate galleon that had fired the cannonball had turned slowly around and was following her.

Jemima was asleep when *The Plunderer* finally pulled silently alongside. She awoke with a jolt to the sound of a sudden shout as a great net swooped down through the air and scooped her up.

Grabbed by the scruff of the neck, Jemima found herself staring into the sneering face of a fierce sea dog. It was a face she had seen before and she was frightened. It belonged to Mad Dog McNasty, notorious pirate captain of *The Plunderer* and well-known bone thief.

His dastardly sea dog crew crowded around Jemima, growling horribly and bearing their terrible teeth.

"Caught you at last, my little sleeping beauty!" growled McNasty. "We need a cat to deal with the shipload of stowaways we've got in the bilges. You take care of our unwanted guests double-quick or I'll take care of you — with pleasure!"

And with a cruel laugh, the captain flung Jemima down into the dark hold.

The hatch lid slammed shut and Jemima landed with a crash among a pile of pirate booty. As her eyes grew accustomed to the gloom, she realized that the hold was full of rats who cowered in every corner, desperately trying to hide.

Now Jemima quite liked rats — fish was her favorite food — but she had a hard time convincing them.

"Listen," she said eventually, "do you really think I'd do McNasty's dirty work? That cut-throat pirate destroyed my boat!"

The leader of the rats, Crooktail, edged forward.

"Then please help us," he begged. "We're starving. There's no food aboard except bones and dog biscuits and both are constantly guarded by Slobber, the ship's cook. If we don't get some food soon, or escape, we're sure to die."

"Why, those sea dogs are nothing to be frightened of," said Jemima bravely. "They're just a bunch of bone thieves. And there's a fine reward for their capture if my memory serves me well. If we put our heads together we can surely think of a plan to escape — and maybe claim a reward in the bargain!"

A few days later McNasty gathered the crew together in his cabin. Little did he know that Jemima and Crooktail were watching through a hole in the wall.

Carefully, he unrolled an ancient treasure map and spread it before him on the table. It showed a small island.

"X marks the spot!" shouted the captain, plunging his dagger into the parchment. "The biggest bones in the world are buried here! We'll dig them up and live like kings. And any ship that dare comes near, why, we'll simply BLAST it out of the water!" The pirates barked and howled with glee.

Jemima and Crooktail looked at each other in dismay. They needed a plan and they needed it fast — otherwise they would be stranded on a desert island for the rest of their days!

For several more days *The Plunderer* sailed on. Meanwhile, Jemima paced the hold trying to think of a plan. And, just as the island came into sight on the horizon, she thought of one.

"A wishbone!" she cried. "With so many bones on board, there's bound to be a wishbone among them, and that's all we need!" The rats looked mystified so Jemima explained.

"When I was a tiny kitten, a wise old cat took me aside and whispered something very special in my ear."

"What?" cried the rats in unison.

"Why, a wishbone wishing spell, of course," said Jemima smiling.

At last, *The Plunderer* anchored in a sheltered bay. Most of the pirates jumped into the rowing boats and rowed eagerly ashore, leaving only a skeleton crew to guard the ship.

In the ship's galley, Slobber was busy boiling bones for the evening meal. Bending down to stir the cooking pot, he didn't see Jemima and the rats creeping up behind him.

Taken by complete surprise, he was soon lying on the floor, bound and gagged, his muffled cries of "Mutiny!" heard only by Jemima and the rats.

Searching quickly through Slobber's huge pile of
bones, Jemima soon found what she was looking
for — a wishbone! She and Crooktail held it
between them and recited the magic wishing
spell she had learned all those years ago:

> *"Our magic wishbone wish will make*
> *These old bones on the floor awake,*
> *And join up once again, we say,*
> *And no one else but us obey!"*

And as they spoke, the bones began to rattle,
rising up from the floor with a loud clatter to
form a series of bony creatures.

"Now we have our own skeleton crew,"
laughed Jemima. "Let's put them to work!"

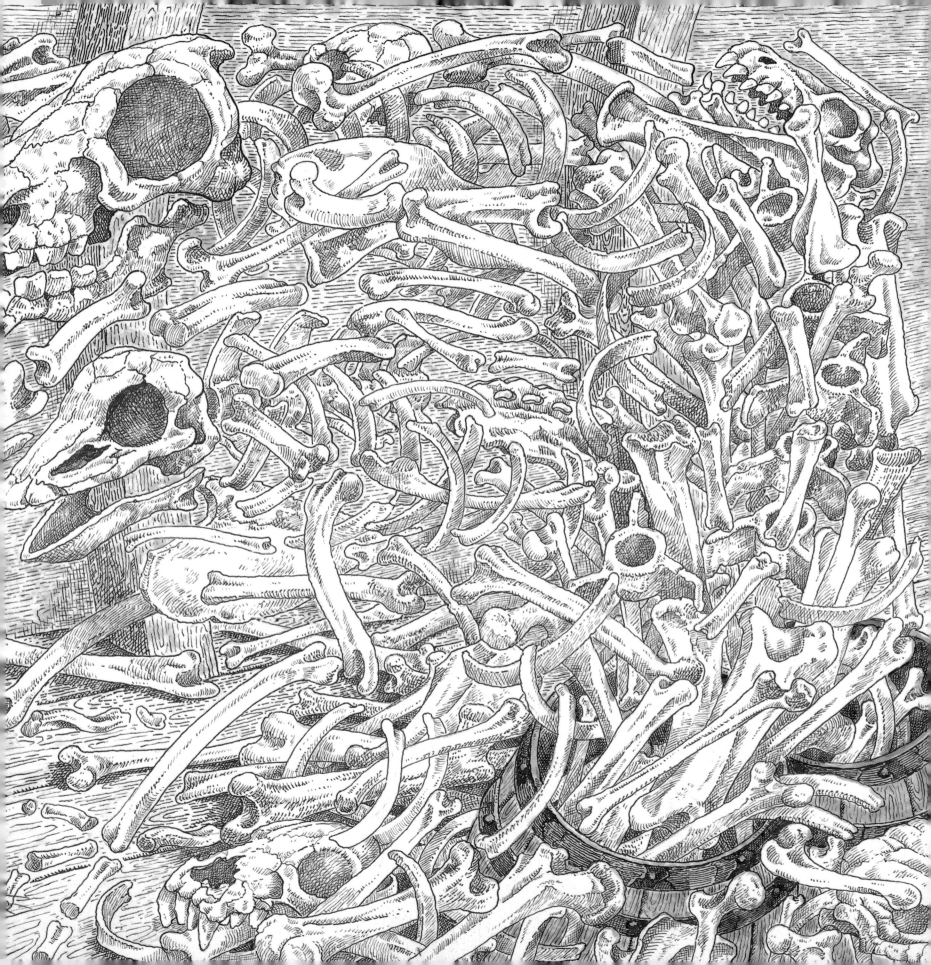

The remaining pirates were playing cards on deck when the skeletons sprang out of the galley. Scattering in terror, the sea dogs tried to escape but it was useless. In no time at all they had all been captured and tied, quivering, to the mast.

Leaving the skeletons to guard the ship, Jemima and the rats lowered a dingy into the water and rowed ashore. They soon found Mad Dog McNasty's heavy footprints and set off to follow the pirates' trail as it wound away from the beach and into a thick jungle.

By the time Jemima caught up with the pirates, they were already hard at work, digging up the most enormous bones. Jemima and the rats settled down to watch and, by late afternoon, the pirates had uncovered the complete skeleton of a huge creature.

It was time for the wishbone to weave its magic once again! Holding it between them, Jemima and Crooktail recited the wishbone spell and, to their delight, the bones rose into the air, rattling together to form a gigantic animal — an ancient dinosaur that towered above the terrified pirates gnashing its terrible teeth.

At Jemima's command, the dinosaur snapped up each and every pirate. They bounced one by one down its bony throat to find themselves trapped, bruised and battered, in its vast rib cage.

Sitting down to pick its teeth with a stray cutlass, the dinosaur waited while Jemima and the rats gathered food and water. As the sun began to set, they all returned to *The Plunderer* where Crooktail lowered the *Jolly Roger* flag for good and, at last, they set sail for home.

With the help of their skeleton crew, it didn't take Jemima and the rats long to reach her home port. They sailed triumphantly into the harbor where Mad Dog McNasty and his sea dogs were soon dispatched to the local prison and put safely behind bars. They had a very long sentence to serve!

With their share of the reward, Crooktail and the rest of the rats bought a little fish shop near the harbor. Jemima knew exactly how she was going to spend her share of the bounty. The very next morning she went out and bought another fishing boat. She called it *Flipper 2* and went on to catch a good deal of fish in it — so many in fact that she gave most of them to the rats to sell. And, with some exciting adventures along the way, they all did very well!